marvelous & kind Kloey

D1378942

Kathy L. Guthrie   Danielle N. Seago

ISBN-13: 978-0692177709
ISBN-10: 0692177701

Dedicated to Kinley and Zoey.
May you always be marvelous and kind!

Hi, my name
is Kloey!

Greetings from

UNIVERSE CITY

I live in Universe City!
We love it here because there's a great view of
earth; so we can see those who we can help!

It's such a fun place to live!

We even have a store
where we buy our hero gear.

And this is my neighborhood.
My house is in the middle!

I'm so lucky my friends live next door to me!

Their names are Violet and Rose.

When we're together, we laugh a lot!

This is my mom and dad. They're pretty great!

My dad builds the best forts!

He teaches what's right and wrong at my school.

My mom
has awesome
dance moves!

She's the
mayor of
Universe City.

I'm so excited you're here with me today because it's my first time to fly on my own!

I really hope I don't fall.

I wonder if Violet and Rose
are as excited as I am!

This is Coach,
    our flying teacher!

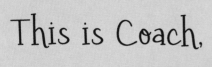

Today is our first day without using
the training birds.

I knew they wouldn't let me fall.

First, Coach reminds us the correct way to fly.

Rose is next.

First, she falls.

She tries again, and she flies!

On our way home, Violet and Rose want to help me practice flying.

"That's ok, I don't want help," I tell them.

At home, Mom and Dad ask how my day was. After telling them I fell... a lot, they ask if they can help.

"Thanks, Mom and Dad,"
I say, "but I don't want any help."

The next day at school,
I fall again.

"Can you help
me, Coach?"

"Yes!"

At least I'm not the only one who can't fly yet.

Wow!

He did it with Coach's help!

ding

I decide to ask for help too.

Coach shows me how to jump high.

Then, I ask Violet and Rose for help,
and they show me how to keep my arms straight.

Last, I ask my mom and dad for help.
They show me how to keep my chin up.

I'm glad I asked for help.
I feel so lucky to have such
marvelous and kind people around me.

I want to be like them and
help others too, because
that's what **heroes** do. ♡

About the Creators

Kathy L Guthrie is a professor at Florida State University who earned her Ph.D. at the University of Illinois at Urbana-Champaign. She resides in Tampa with her husband and daughter, affectionately known as Team Guthrie.

Danielle N. Seago is a graphic designer and illustrator who earned her Bachelor's of Science in Mass Communications from Southern Illinois University Edwardsville. She resides in Central Illinois with her husband, Greg, and daughter, Zoey.